10c

4/08

An Anancy Spiderman Story

FIRST PALM TREES

BY James Berry

ILLUSTRATED BY Greg Couch

Simon & Schuster
Books for Young Readers

t that time, no palm trees were in the world. Not one palm tree was anywhere.

One morning, Priest Ajayee said to the king, "You know, Your Majesty, last night I had a most pleasant dream. I dreamed some new and beautiful trees—plume trees that give wine—were growing on your land." The king smiled. "It's a most magnificent tree, Sire. It has a straight and clean trunk with branches like a peacock's tail. It lingers in my head it may be called a 'palm tree,' which gives 'plume wine' or 'palm wine.'"

The king was excited. "A wine tree? *You* are my dream prophet! You dreamed of wine-giving trees on *my* land. Your dreams have always worked. Your dreams take you beyond nights and days. They take you and show you hidden times, and hidden places, and their magic. My priest, my wise man, how will it happen? Will you get the help of Tree-Spirit? And Sky-God?"

"Royal Sire, it may happen through one. Or both. Or none direct. I will search out a way long and hard."

The king went silent for a moment and then said, "Priest Ajayee, to the one who makes your dream happen, I will give a reward. A rich reward. My priest, let my promised reward be known among all our people."

As usual, quickly, Anancy Spiderman was among the first to hear about the king's reward. The hope of a rich reward went to his head instantly, taking charge of him. Anancy walked about, thinking, thinking. He was certain he was the right, proper, and best person to receive the king's reward.

Anancy came out into open land. He leaned against a big round rock. Anancy was full of thinking how he must talk to Sky-God. Must be the first—the very first—to reach Sky-God.

And, unexpectedly, *plipss!* Beside him, a slant of dazzling rainbow light floated. The slanted Sun-Spirit stayed still, floating, hanging in the air. A most unbelievable presence. And soon Anancy heard Sun-Spirit's voice. It was a thin, clear, high-pitched sound that asked, "What is it you want done, Anancy?"

"Well," Anancy said, "I have a job. A *great great* job. We'll share the reward. A fantastic reward. Given by the king."

Sun-Spirit's thin, high-pitched voice asked, "What is the work?"

"To make palm trees. A field of them. A whole field. On the king's own land. Can you do that?"

"Yes."

"Good news come! Good news come!"

"Then I'll get my partner to talk to you."

"Partner?" Anancy was shocked. "Partner, you said? What partner? It's a job for one worker only. Shared out, my reward will be in pieces. I want one worker only."

"My work is not only my work," Sun-Spirit said simply.

nancy knew he had to be quick. He had to use his persuasive sweet-talking. "Sun alone melts the seas of ice." Anancy was calm. "Sun alone melts frozen lands. And makes them warm and green and fruitful and rich. You are Sky-God's eye. Your eye sees everything and finds anything. You don't need a partner."

"My work is not only my work," Sun-Spirit said again.

Anancy was insistent. "Sun-Spirit, Sun-Spirit," he said. "Get this work done, alone, for me—for me and our king—and I'll get your sun-eye to shine and shine and stay shining all through one night *every every* year, everywhere. And have everybody—everybody—singing and feasting and dancing, praising the light of your eye."

"My work makes other works work," Sun-Spirit said. "And other works make my work also work. On my own I cannot make one root, one leaf, one blossom, one fruit. Say now. Is it to be my partnership and all work? Or is it to be no work at all?" Sun-Spirit was ready to leave. In that thin voice, the final words came. "Speak your last word, Anancy. Partnership or not?"

Anancy winced. He felt himself on the brink of losing everything. Two now! *Two*—to share the reward! Yet—why worry? After all—wasn't he able to fix things and make them come right? Wasn't he called "Mr. Anancy," "Father Anancy," "Trickster," and "Spider," who'd run up a thread or a tree and collect Sky-God's good and bad messages? "Partnership," he said. "Partnership."

Plipss! Sun-Spirit was gone. Disappeared.

Straightaway, *schwaah!* Where Sun-Spirit had stood, Water-Spirit now stood. Like tall majestic strands of silver wire, Water-Spirit was shining strings of rain. Wonderfully bundled and brilliantly gleaming. In a voice that was a musical gargle, Water-Spirit asked, "What is it you want done, Anancy?"

"I want some palm trees made. Urgent! Urgent! A *great great* job to make one other person rich with me. Palm trees to be made on the king's own land. *Sure sure* you can make palm trees on the king's own land!"

"Yes," Water-Spirit said.

"Good news come! Good news come!"

"Then I'll get my partner to talk to you."

Shocked as before, Anancy said, "Partner? We don't need a partner at all. It's a job for one worker only." Anancy wondered how he could persuade out a single-worker deal. He begged. "Water-Spirit. Please. Do. Take on this job alone. If you need a helper, make that your own business, separately. Then I share the reward with just you."

"My work is not only my work," Water-Spirit said calmly.

ut, alone, your driving power of rain filled the seas. Without you a place is barren land. Your rush of rain tramples a desert and flowers bloom. Alone, you make green leaves rush out into life, sticking to stems and branches. You don't need a partner."

"My work is not only my work. It must be all partnership. With you as well."

Anancy went on with his pleading again. "Water-Spirit, Water-Spirit, get the work done, alone, for me—for me and our king—and after every rainfall—every rainfall—I'll get all toads, all frogs, all crickets, all birds to sing praises—sing praises—to water, half a day! On and on, half a day!"

"My work makes other works work," Water-Spirit said. "Other works make my work also work. On my own I cannot make one root, one leaf, one blossom, one fruit. Is it to be my partnership and all work? Or is it to be no work at all?" And in that musical gargle of a voice Water-Spirit ended, "Speak your last word, Anancy. Partnership or not?"

Again that word "partnership" was a terrible obstacle for Anancy. This was agony. Three now! Three—to share it. Yet—why worry? Didn't he know he possessed extra senses to find ways to fix the reward—or anything—in the end? "Partnership," he said. "Partnership."

Schwaah! Water-Spirit disappeared. Was gone.

Goomsh! And where Water-Spirit had stood, Earth-Spirit now stood. Earth-Spirit was an amazing mound of glittering earth. All glittery and starry, Earth-Spirit looked like a beautifully rounded pile of crushed black, brown, and white diamonds. And in a voice that was a gentle echoing rumble, Earth-Spirit asked, "What is it you want done, Anancy?"

Anancy explained. Then he asked, "Can you do the job, Earth-Spirit? Can you make palm trees? On the king's own land?"

"Yes."

Anancy hopped two steps of a little jig. "Oh, good news come! Good news come!"

"Then I'll get my partner to talk to you."

The amazing Mr. Anancy now pretended to be as shocked as ever. Looking deeply serious, he pleaded. "This is a job for a single worker only. Only one. Get it done single-handed and *you alone* will share the reward with me. You alone!"

"My work is not only my work," Earth-Spirit said calmly.

nancy turned on his sweet-talking. "As wide as the sky," he gestured, "earth is solid. You are big. You are everything. You are the bosom of roots and rocks and every ocean and sea. On you, every foot and flight lands. You make food for every tooth, tongue, and belly. You provide sleeping place, nesting place, hiding place for all you care for. Every tree is settled in you. All tree secrets are in you. All secrets are in you to make a tree—alone!"

"My work is not only my work."

"Earth-Spirit, Earth-Spirit, get the work done, alone, for me and our king, and on every high hill I'll have flowers blooming— flowers white and red and yellow and blue, from top to bottom all around every hill—blooming with a show for every eye, for praises for you from every lip."

"My work makes other works work," Earth-Spirit said. "Other works make my work also work. On my own I cannot make one root, one leaf, one blossom, one fruit. Is it to be my partnership and all work? Or is it to be no work at all?" Ready to leave, Earth-Spirit, in a gentle echoing rumble, finished, "Speak your last word, Anancy. Partnership or not?"

Again, this "partnership" business was a *bad bad* trial. Four now to share the reward. Four! Yet—why worry? Didn't he possess ten smart senses to make him get above, under, around, and through a situation? Why should getting *all* the reward be different? "Partnership," he said. "Partnership."

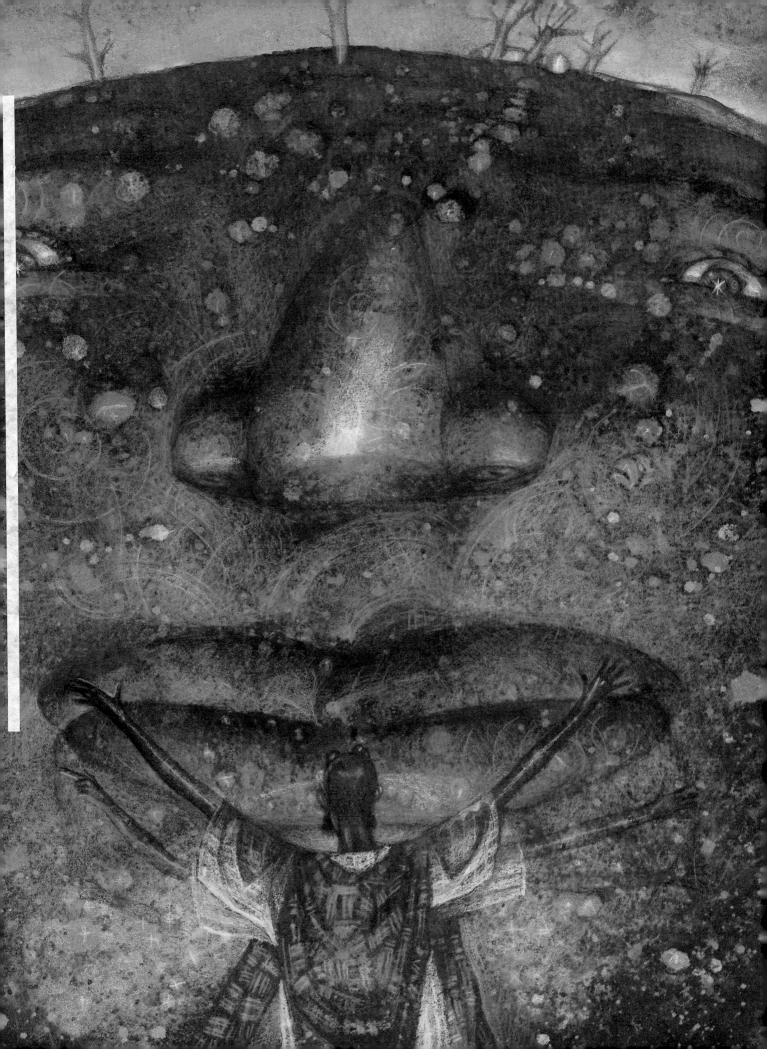

Goomsh! Earth-Spirit disappeared. Was gone.

Swoosch! And where Earth-Spirit had stood, Air-Spirit now stood. An upright flappy pool of wind, this! Magnificent, transparent, mysterious, all blowy with a shimmer! And, in a clear, whistly voice, a clean voice, Air-Spirit asked, "What is it you want done, Anancy?"

Anancy explained how he urgently wanted somebody to make palm trees and share a reward with him. A fantastic reward! Given by the king. Could Air-Spirit do the job? Could Air-Spirit make palm trees on the king's own land?

"Yes."

"Good news come!" Anancy said. "Good news come!"

"Then, we've all talked to you now," Air-Spirit said. "I am the fourth partner. All four of us work together. With you now, our caller-to-work. We could call you our fifth partner."

nancy whispered to himself, "Four of them! Four! My reward will be in tatters." Much, much better to deal with that trouble now. He had to throw himself into one last crafty fling to get that single-worker only.

"Air-Spirit, Air-Spirit," he said. "You are in charge of everywhere. A worker of worldwide experience, working by yourself, air is never lonely." And Anancy's voice became most persuasive now. "Get the work done. Make palm trees, *alone*, for me and our king. And on special days every year, I'll get your unseen feathery self of air, spreading around cities and towns, full of the scents of crushed sandalwood and cinnamon and dried sweet herbs. The *sweet sweet* scents you carry will wash everyone. And everyone will sing and sing praises and praises to you."

"My work makes other works work," Air-Spirit said. "Other works make my work also work. On my own I cannot make one root, one leaf, one blossom, one fruit. Is it to be my partnership and all work? Or is it to be no work at all?" Obviously ready to leave, Air-Spirit, in that clear and clean whistly voice, finished, "Speak your last word, Anancy."

Anancy knew he had to—*had to*—give in to this "partnership" business. "Partnership," he said. "Partnership."

Swoosch! Air-Spirit disappeared. Was gone.

Anancy had no idea whether anything would happen or not. But Anancy went on as if he well understood everything. A couple of days later, to get himself seen and to create mystery and excitement, he walked into a group of village elders. All showed instant interest in Anancy.

"So, like others have," an elder said, "we hear you have put in your claim to the priest for the king's plume tree reward."

All nodded. "Yes, yes. We've all heard."

Another elder said, "Where, then, will we see this plume tree growing? And when?"

Anancy gave away nothing. He said, "I'm busy with it. Busy. Busy! If you don't see me around I could be up, could be down, could be under the sea or over it, searching."

Time passed, and Anancy heard nothing. He asked Sky-God why there was no news about his work with Sun, Water, Earth, and Air-Spirits. No answer came. For days he talked to Sky-God when he walked about, sat still, or lay down. And there was no answer whatsoever. Anancy decided he would try to get a sign from either Sun, Water, Earth, or Air-Spirit directly.

One time, another time, many times, he sat out
in the sun, feeling the sun's heat, listening, looking,
waiting, thinking hard, and received no sign from
Sun-Spirit whatsoever.

One time, another time, many times, thinking
hard, he walked about in the pelting rain, swam
about in the river, stood in the middle of it, sat
with his legs in it, and received no sign from
Water-Spirit whatsoever.

One time, another time, many times, thinking
hard, he lay flat on the bare earth, stood in a hole
in the ground, covered himself with earth, and
received no sign from Earth-Spirit whatsoever.

One time, another time, many times, thinking
hard, he walked backward and forward in strong
wind, stayed out all night in the night air, and
received no sign from Air-Spirit whatsoever.

Anancy was painfully impatient and anxious.
Were his contacts really working on the palm
trees? Would they win him the reward? And would
those workers show themselves and prove his win?

One morning Anancy slept late. His son, Tacooma, woke him up. Anancy was surprised to find it was midday. "Get up!" Tacooma said. "All the village has gone to see the palm trees."

Anancy and Tacooma began to run. Finally they came to the king's land. The field was full of new plumed trees. Together, Anancy and Tacooma hurried toward the palace to collect the king's reward.

The king was on the palace grounds with the priest and village elders and a crowd of other people. Excited groups of villagers walked about, pointing at all sizes of the new plume-limbed trees. Some people stood spellbound, while others chatted noisily.

Anancy, with Tacooma, walked up to the king and Priest Ajayee. Lots of other special people were around the king, gazing at him, listening to him.

When the king stopped speaking, a special person said, "Sire—a medicine man. I registered for the reward. I worked for it. And just as we medicine men bring new health, I summoned plume-limbed trees from dreamland to our king's land." A big roar of the crowd acknowledged him.

Another special person said to the king, "Sire—a rainmaker. I registered for the reward. I worked for it. And just as we rainmakers call rain from the sky, I called plume-limbed trees up from the ground onto our king's land." A big roar of the crowd acknowledged him.

Another special person said to the king, "Sire—a speaker to spirits. I registered for the reward. I worked for it. And just as we mediums bring news from spirit worlds, in my state of a trance I saw the trees. I requested their transfer onto our king's land." A big roar of the crowd acknowledged her.

Anancy said to the king, "Sire—Anancy. You needed. I needed. We needed. I asked. And Sun-Spirit, Water-Spirit, Earth-Spirit, Air-Spirit all made the trees." A big roar of the crowd acknowledged Anancy.

The king raised his arms. The crowd was silenced. He said, "Altogether, thirty are claiming my reward. Thirty! Which one is the actual getter of our palm trees? Which one should be the receiver of my reward? It could be any one. But no one has proved the bringing of the trees. No one has shown the work in the bringing of the trees. And I do see that the new trees belong to everybody. So my gesture of a reward is toward everyone. Instead of a single reward, I invite all here—everybody—to a feasting with me. Now!"

The voices were thunderous. "Hurrah! hurrah! hurrah! for the king! Hurrah! hurrah! hurrah! for the king!"

Everyone knew. Everyone well understood all happened because of Anancy. They knew that without Anancy—without the spider hero and his magical personality—the big spirits would not have taken on the palm trees job. They believed that without him, the worker spirits would not even have heard the call for palm trees. Yet, while he still stood or walked or sat anywhere, nobody, nobody had any intention to admit Anancy caused it.

Walking home, Anancy and Tacooma noticed palm trees were now everywhere, on almost everybody's land. Like people newly arrived, the trees waved happily in the little wind. And they belonged to everyone. Yet it was a long, long time after it happened before everyone began to say, "Anancy brought palm trees to the people! Anancy brought palm trees to the people! Anancy . . . Anancy . . . Anancy . . ."

For my brother, Ben
—JB

For my mother, Marilyn
—GC

Author's note

I've always been interested in Anancy. He's the most popular mythical character who has come from Africa to the Caribbean and lives in a literary form. And though Anancy is a trickster, his cosmic self always brings something to his people: Sometimes it is something bad; sometimes it is something good. When I got the idea for this tale, I was really excited. I knew it would give me the chance to develop some of Anancy's usual characteristics and situations into an original story.

—James Berry

Illustrator's note

After reading a piece by James Berry about the nature of Anancy—who is essentially both man and spider at the same time—I decided to portray Anancy as a man with spidery characteristics. So I gave him eight eyes (his own plus three pairs of glasses) and eight arms (suggested by his motions and the folds of his robe) to symbolize the eight eyes and arms of a spider.

I also based many of the patterns in the illustrations for *First Palm Trees* on African *kente* cloth patterns. Traditionally kente cloths usually said something about the wearer. Certain weaves could be worn only by men, others only by women or by people of certain standing in the community with the king's permission. Weaves were created to honor great deeds, events, or people and to symbolize things in nature.

In *First Palm Trees*, the weave the king wears at the end of the story is called "liar's cloth"; it was worn only by kings when settling claims made by people who might not be telling the truth. In the middle of the story, the stripe that appears in the sky when Anancy appeals to Sky-God for news is from a weave called "the Sky God's arch." The pattern in Sun-Spirit's light is based on a weave called "unity is strength" because Sun-Spirit is the first one to declare that creating palm trees must be a cooperative effort. Anancy is dressed in a weave that would be worn by a commoner.

—Greg Couch

HOW THE ART WAS CREATED:

I start with an acrylic wash on museum board, a very thick watercolor paper. Often I build up several layers of washes. Then I draw people or objects and add details with Derwent studio colored pencils. If the details need to be more colorful, I use a small paintbrush and more acrylics to brighten them up. I lighten areas of the background in many of the illustrations with Comet cleanser, which bleaches out previous layers of paint; it's something I discovered by accident one day and have enjoyed using ever since. In other illustrations I create a textured effect using a plant mister and/or table salt.

SIMON & SCHUSTER BOOKS FOR YOUNG READERS An imprint of Simon & Schuster Children's Publishing Division
1230 Avenue of the Americas, New York, New York 10020. Text copyright © 1997 by James Berry. Illustrations copyright © 1997 by Greg Couch.
SIMON & SCHUSTER BOOKS FOR YOUNG READERS is a trademark of Simon & Schuster.
Book design by Paul Zakris. The text of this book is set in 15-point Block regular. Printed and bound in the United States of America.
First Edition 10 9 8 7 6 5 4 3 2 1

LIBRARY OF CONGRESS CATALOGING-IN-PUBLICATION DATA
Berry, James.
   First palm trees / by James Berry ; illustrated by Greg Couch. — 1st ed.
      p. cm.
   Summary: The West Indian trickster Anancy Spiderman tries to persuade Sun-Spirit, Water-Spirit, Earth-Spirit, and Air-Spirit to create the world's first palm trees so that he can collect a reward from the king.
   ISBN 0-689-81060-1
   1. Anansi (Legendary character)—Legends. [1. Anansi (Legendary character)—Legends. 2. Folklore—West Indies.] I. Couch, Greg, ill. II. Title.
PZ8.1.B4187Fi 1997 398.24′52544—dc20 [E] 96-24618 CIP AC